A SLED DOG FOR MOSHI

Jeanne Bushey

Illustrated by Germaine Arnaktauyok

Fitzhenry & Whiteside

Published in paperback by Fitzhenry & Whiteside in 2005
Originally published by Hyperion Press Limited in 1994

Published in Canada by Fitzhenry & Whiteside,
195 Allstate Parkway, Markham, Ontario L3R 4T8

Published in the United States by Fitzhenry & Whiteside,
121 Harvard Avenue, Suite 2, Allston, Massachusetts 02134

www.fitzhenry.ca   godwit@fitzhenry.ca

10 9 8 7 6 5 4 3 2 1

Library and Archives Canada Cataloguing in Publication
Bushey, Jeanne, 1944-
A sled dog for Moshi / Jeanne Bushey ; illustrated by Germaine Arnaktauyok.
First published: Winnipeg : Hyperion Press, 1994.
ISBN 1-55041-956-0
1. Inuit—Canada—Juvenile fiction. 2. Sled dogs—Juvenile fiction.
I. Arnaktauyok, Germaine II. Title.
PS8553.U69654S54 2005   jC813'.54   C2005-904348-2

**U.S. Publisher Cataloging-in-Publication Data
(Library of Congress Standards)**

Bushey, Jeanne.
A sled dog for Moshi / Jeanne Bushey ; illustrated by Germaine Arnaktauyok.
Originally published: New York, N.Y. : Hyperion Books for Children,   c1994.
[40] p. : col. ill. ; cm.
Summary: Moshi would like a small dog like her friend Jessica has, then one day
during a snowstorm Moshi realizes the benefit of having a sled dog of her own.
ISBN 1-55041-956-0 (pbk.)
1. Eskimos — Juvenile fiction. (1. Eskimos — Fiction. 2. Dogs — Fiction.
3. Pets — Fiction. 4. Snow — Fiction.) I. Arnaktauyok, Germaine, ill. II. Title.
[E] dc22   PZ7.B96546Sl 2005

Fitzhenry & Whiteside acknowledges with thanks the Canada Council for the Arts,
the Government of Canada through the Book Publishing Industry Development Program (BPIDP),
and the Ontario Arts Council for their support of our publishing program.

Canada Council   Conseil des Arts
for the Arts   du Canada

ONTARIO ARTS COUNCIL
CONSEIL DES ARTS DE L'ONTARIO

Paperback cover design by Wycliffe Smith

Printed in Hong Kong

FINLAND
Baltic Sea
SWEDEN
NORWAY
Norwegian Sea
No
SCOTLA
IRELA
ICELAND
ATLANTIC OCEAN

ARCTIC OCEAN
North Pole
Arctic Circle
RUSSIA
GREENLAND
Arctic Circle
Baffin Bay
Baffin Island
Iqaluit
Beaufort Sea

Bering Sea
Aleutian Islands
Alaska U.S.A.
PACIFIC OCEAN

Hudson Bay
C A N A D A

NewYork

U N I T E D   S T A T E S

"I wish I had a dog like Tippy," Moshi said as she held her friend Jessica's new puppy in her arms. She gave the small white terrier a quick hug before handing him back to Jessica.

"Don't you have your own dog?" Jessica asked. "I saw lots of dogs in the pen beside your house."

"Those are my dad's sled dogs," Moshi said. "Inuit dogs aren't pets. They're used for racing mostly, although some of the men in our village still use dog teams, instead of snowmobiles, for hunting."

"If you had a sled dog for a pet, he could take us for rides," Jessica exclaimed. "And I'm sure we could teach him to do tricks the way Tippy can."

Moshi was not surprised that Jessica did not understand about sled dogs. Jessica was from New York City and had moved to the remote northern village of Iqaluit only a few months ago.

Moshi watched Tippy dancing on his hind feet. He seemed so clever! Inuit dogs could only pull sleds. More than anything in the world Moshi wanted a dog like Tippy.

"Our lead dog's going to have pups soon," Moshi announced. "Maybe I could have one of them." She brushed her hair back from her face. "I'm going to ask my dad for one as soon as I get home."

When Moshi walked in the back door of her house, she found her father standing in the middle of the kitchen. Melting snow dripped from his sealskin boots, called kamiks, onto the floor. His mittened hand held a pail of frozen fish for the dogs.

"Nuna's gone," her father said angrily. "I went out to feed the dogs, and she wasn't there!"

"Don't worry," Moshi's mother said gently as she held Moshi's youngest brother on her lap. "She'll be back in the morning when she's hungry. You've had dogs get away before."

Her father frowned. "I don't want anything to happen to her. She's my best dog, and her pups will be born soon. Those pups will be worth a lot of money someday."

"Do we have to sell all the pups this time?" Moshi blurted out.

Her father looked puzzled. "I might keep one or two for my team. Why do you ask, little one?"

Moshi looked up and said, "I would like one for a pet. Like Jessica's new puppy."

"Ah, so you want a plaything dog like your friend has," Moshi's father said quietly. "Her little dog is so small it could be a cat. Nuna's pups won't be like that. They will grow into strong sled dogs, not dogs that do tricks." He sighed. "I'm sorry, but it would be a waste of a good dog."

Moshi was disappointed, but she hoped her father might change his mind once Nuna returned. When several days passed and still the dog had not come home, Moshi felt sad for her father. She knew that Nuna was his favorite.

Every afternoon when school was over, Moshi and Jessica played with Tippy. They dressed him in a doll's sweater and took him outside, where he walked warily across the snowy ground. When Tippy got cold, they brought him inside and rolled his ball for him to chase. Moshi thought Tippy was the smartest dog she had ever seen.

The following week spring returned to Iqaluit. The sun shone with real warmth for the first time since the long, cold winter had ended. The snow began to melt, and water ran in wide streams along the gravelly earth. Tiny flowers sprang up in patches among the rocks, dotting the tundra with color.

On Saturday the girls sat on the steps outside Jessica's house. "Tippy can't play outside today. He'd get too dirty in all this mud," Jessica said. "How about going exploring instead?" She pointed to a high ridge behind her house. "We could go up on those rocks."

The girls climbed to the top of the ridge, where they could see far out over the frozen bay. They watched the changing shadows on the ice made by small clouds drifting across the sun. Jessica climbed over the ridge and started down toward the bay, picking handfuls of fluffy white blossoms that grew among the rocks.

"What are these flowers called?" Jessica asked. "They look just like dandelions."

"They're called arctic cotton," Moshi replied, climbing down after her friend. "But you won't find many flowers down by the ice. Let's go home now. I'm hungry."

Moshi shivered as a cold wind blew in from the bay. She looked up at the sky and saw that the sun was hidden behind a thickening layer of gray clouds. The warm spring day had disappeared. "It's going to snow. We'd better hurry," she urged.

"That's crazy," Jessica laughed. "It doesn't snow in May!"

"That's not true here," Moshi said. "When there's a whiteout it snows so much, you can't even see where you're going. It can come out of nowhere this time of year." She turned back the way they had come.

Snowflakes began to fall, and the ground was quickly covered with a thick layer of white. The wind blew fiercely from all directions, and the falling snow stung like sharp stones as it struck the girls' faces.

"Moshi, wait!" Jessica called anxiously. "I can hardly see you anymore."

Moshi shielded her eyes from the snow. She grabbed one of Jessica's bare hands. "Where are your mittens?" she asked with concern.

"I didn't bring any," Jessica answered. "I didn't know it was going to snow!"

"Here, wear one of mine. Keep your other hand in your pocket," Moshi said. "It'll help a little." She strained to see ahead. "I think this is the way, over here."

Moshi pulled Jessica along behind her. She now had no sense of where they were. She couldn't see anything. The howling wind blocked out all other sounds. She knew stories of people who got turned around in whiteouts and walked in the wrong direction.

Without warning, a large, dark shape jumped up against Moshi's chest. "Nuna," Moshi exclaimed as she blinked the snow away from her eyes. The dog whined as Moshi shook Jessica's arm and cried, "It's Nuna, our lead dog!" Then Nuna tugged on the sleeve of Moshi's parka. "I think she wants us to come with her," Moshi said.

The girls followed along behind the dog. Nuna ran ahead and then returned, barking sharply.

As they stumbled through the driving snow, they could barely see the small shed that appeared in front of them. Nuna barked again and crawled through a hole in the skirting around the base of the building. Moshi and Jessica followed on their hands and knees. Underneath the shed they were safe from the storm.

"Brush off your clothes," Moshi said. "If the snow melts on you and then freezes again, you'll be even colder." She carefully wiped all traces of snow off her own parka and turned to help Jessica.

"Where are we?" Jessica asked. "Why did Nuna bring us here?"

"I think this is one of the storage sheds on the edge of town where we keep frozen meat and fish," Moshi answered. "But I don't know why Nuna took us here instead of home."

As their eyes adjusted to the dim light, Jessica and Moshi looked toward Nuna on the far side of the building. Nuna lay on her side, surrounded by a wriggling mass of fur. Moshi crawled toward the dog. "Jessica, look!" she cried. "Nuna's pups! That's why she didn't take us home. She has her pups under here!"

Moshi touched the nearest little head. The pup turned toward her, his eyes still closed. He pressed his cold nose into the palm of her hand. "I'll name you Siku," Moshi laughed. "That means 'ice,' and your nose is as cold as ice."

Carefully Jessica picked up a second puppy. "They're so cute," she said.

Moshi reached over to pet Nuna, who stretched out her head and licked Moshi's hand. A yellow plastic rope was tied around her neck. Its broken end hung down her back. "Look!" Moshi cried. "Someone must have tied her up. I bet they wanted to keep her pups but she broke free. I guess she couldn't get home in time to give birth so she stopped here." Moshi stroked the fur on Nuna's head.

"I'm glad Nuna found us," Jessica said, "but how are we going to get home?" She buried her face in her puppy's fur and started to cry.

"Please don't cry, Jessica," Moshi said as she wiped away Jessica's tears with her mittened hand. "Your tears will freeze! Any three-year-old Inuk knows that!" she said, shaking her head.

Moshi reached into her pocket. "Look, we've even got food! Here's some bannock my mother baked this morning." Moshi divided the circle of bread with her friend. "Maybe we shouldn't eat it all right now. There's no telling how long the storm's going to last."

As the girls huddled together, Nuna approached Moshi, then barked and darted outside. Both girls turned to watch the hole, but the dog did not return.

"She's running away again!" Jessica wailed. "Now what will we do?"

"She didn't run away in the first place. She would never do that," Moshi said sharply, defending the dog. "We'll just have to wait here with the pups until the storm is over," she added more patiently.

The girls huddled next to the puppies. After a few minutes Jessica fell asleep, but Moshi stayed awake and listened to the storm outside. As the light under the building faded almost completely, Moshi knew that the afternoon had passed. Soon it would be dark and very cold under the shed.

The roar of snowmobiles interrupted her thoughts. Moshi heard a dog barking and men calling.

"Jessica, wake up!" Moshi cried. "Someone's coming!"

It seemed as if everything happened at once. Nuna bounded through the hole, barking loudly. Moshi's father peered under the building. He saw the girls and shouted, "They're here. They're all right!" Moshi and Jessica climbed out through the hole. Moshi's father hugged both girls tightly. The other men helped carry the pups out.

"Nuna saved us!" Moshi said, looking at the big dog with a new appreciation for her abilities. "Did you see the rope? Someone tried to keep her, but she broke free!"

"The police will check into it later," her father answered. "They've been pretty busy the last few hours looking for two little girls who were foolish enough to go out in a whiteout." He looked sternly down at Moshi while Jessica climbed onto the komatik, the long sled behind the snowmobile. "Your friend doesn't know any better, but you do," he said.

"It's not Moshi's fault," Jessica said. "The whiteout came so fast we couldn't get back from the ridge. If it wasn't for her, I would have frozen. She shared her mittens with me, and she kept me warm when we were under the building."

"I tried to remember the things you taught me when we went camping in the winter," Moshi said, looking up at her father.

"I am proud of you, little one. You thought like an Inuk," her father replied. "But I've been thinking that if you had had a good dog with you today, perhaps this would not have happened. Is there one of Nuna's pups you would like for a pet?"

"Oh, yes," Moshi said. She pointed to Siku. "That is the one I want. But I don't want him to be a pet to do tricks. I want him to be a sled dog, just like his mother."

Arctic   This northern area is one of the coldest regions on earth. Alaska, northern Canada, Greenland, and parts of Russia, Norway, Sweden, and Finland belong to the Arctic region. The Inuit have lived there for thousands of years. Many still live a partly nomadic life, staying in the settled communities for the winter, then moving inland to hunt during the short summer.

komatik   A sled that is about fifteen feet long, with two wooden runners and wooden slats in between. It is lashed with rawhide rather than nailed in order to be more flexible as it bounces over the ice. The first komatiks were made of caribou antlers and driftwood. The runners were often made of frozen mud.

bannock   Flat bread made from flour, fat, salt, water, and baking powder that is similar in flavor to a scone. It can be fried in a pan over an open fire or baked in an oven. It was probably introduced to the Inuit by Scottish and English fur traders and whalers.

Inuit   People who are native to North America's Arctic region are often called Eskimos, but they refer to themselves as Inuit (IN-yuh-wut), meaning "the people." An Inuit person is called an Inuk.

kamiks   Knee-high sealskin or caribou boots with socklike thick woolen liners that are embroidered along the top and folded over the kamik at the knee.

tundra   These regions of the Northern Hemisphere have no trees and an abundant outcropping of rock. In summer flowering dwarf shrubs grow in thin, wet soil that is spread over permanently frozen ground underneath.

whiteout   Weather condition caused by blowing snow that greatly reduces visibility so that the horizon cannot be seen. People in a whiteout often cannot see one foot in front of themselves.